The Berenstain Bears
Lend a Helping Hand

Some cubs are helpful.
Some cubs are not.
Show them the way
and they may take a shot.

A First Time Book®

Random House
New York

www.randomhouse.com/kids/
www.berenstainbears.com

Library of Congress Cataloging-in-Publication Data
Berenstain, Stan, 1923-   The Berenstain Bears lend a helping
hand / Stan & Jan Berenstain.   p. cm. — (First time books)
SUMMARY: Mama Bear hopes to teach the cubs to think of others instead of
only themselves by having them help an elderly neighbor clean out her attic.
ISBN 0-679-88956-6 (trade). — ISBN 0-679-98956-0 (lib. bdg.) [1. Bears—Fiction.
2. Helpfulness—Fiction. 3. Selfishness—Fiction. 4. Brothers and sisters—Fiction.]
I. Berenstain, Jan, 1923-   . II. Title. III. Series: Berenstain, Stan, 1923- .
First time books. PZ7.B4483Bersc 1998 [E]—dc21 98-7367
Printed in the United States of America 10 9 8 7 6 5 4 3 2 1

Mama and Papa Bear were like most parents. They wanted the best for their cubs. Brother and Sister were like most cubs. They wanted the best for themselves—and not only the best, but the biggest and the most as well—

the best place in front of the TV,

the biggest piece of cake,

and the most jellybeans.

One night, when the squabbling cubs were sound asleep, Mama lay awake worrying. She sighed a big sigh.

"Was that a sigh?" asked Papa, turning over. "Or just the wind whistling through the leaves of our tree house?"

"We've got to find a way of teaching Brother and Sister to mend their selfish ways," she said. "Do you have any suggestions?"

But "Z-Z-Z-Z" was Papa's only suggestion. He had fallen asleep, leaving Mama alone with her thoughts.

I've got to find a way, thought Mama, to teach them that it's just as important to help others as it is to help themselves. But how? Lecturing hasn't worked. Nagging hasn't worked. And having Papa "talk" to them seems to do more harm than good.

As Mama lay there, she thought about how cubs learn. Cubs learn by *doing*. They learn to walk by walking. They learn to run by running. They learn to climb by climbing. That's the answer, thought Mama. The cubs will learn to help others by *helping others*. But questions of who, when, and where went unanswered as she drifted off to sleep.

As it happened, those questions would soon be answered. The *who* turned out to be Miz McGrizz, the elderly widow who lived just down the road. The *when* turned out to be the very next day. And the *where* turned out to be at the checkout line at the supermarket.

"Hello, Miz McGrizz," said Mama as she emptied her cart at the checkout counter.

"Hello, yourself," said Miz McGrizz. "How are you and yours?"

"Just fine," said Mama. "Some of mine are over there looking at the videos. Cubs, say hello to our neighbor."

"Hi, Miz McGrizz," said Brother and Sister.

The cubs were a little nervous about Miz McGrizz. She was really old (even older than Gramps and Gran) and kind of bent over. And there was that crookedy cane she used when she walked. But the real reason they were nervous about her was that their ball had gone into her yard and knocked over some tulips. They had never apologized.

When Mama and the cubs were loading their groceries into the car, Miz McGrizz came out of the supermarket pushing her little collapsible shopping cart.

"Where are you going?" called Mama.

"To the bus stop," she said. "The bus goes right by my house."

"So does our car," said Mama.

"Cubs, help Miz McGrizz into the car and put her things in the trunk."

"That's very kind," said Miz McGrizz as Sister helped her into the car. "My goodness," she added as Brother put her things in the trunk, "it must be wonderful to have such helpful cubs."

"Yes, it is," said Mama as she started the car. "Most of the time."

"It certainly would be wonderful for me," said Miz McGrizz.

"Oh?" said Mama. When the cubs realized they were being talked about, they leaned forward to hear better.

"Yes," said Miz McGrizz. "I need a little help with something."

By now Brother and Sister were leaning so far forward that the seat belts were pulling at them.

Hmm, thought Mama, maybe this is the chance I've been looking for—the chance for Brother and Sister to learn to help others.

"I wonder," said Miz McGrizz, "and this is just a thought—but I wonder if perhaps Brother and Sister could find the time to help me clean up my attic—it's an awful mess. I'd pay them, of course." Brother and Sister looked at each other.

They didn't say anything, but their expressions spoke volumes. Help Miz McGrizz clean her attic? What about soccer? What about listening to records with Lizzy? What about playing video games with Cousin Fred?

"Well, I for one think that's a wonderful idea," said Mama. "Cubs, how does next Saturday sound?" She pulled the car in close to Miz McGrizz's house.

"*Next Saturday?*" said the cubs.

"Then it's a deal!" said Mama. "Hop to it, cubs. Let's help Miz McGrizz get her things into the house."

As the cubs helped, they saw next Saturday slipping away in the dusty haze of a miserable, boring old attic.

When they were about to head home, Mama turned to Miz McGrizz. "As for paying Brother and Sister," she said, "they wouldn't *think* of accepting money for being nice to a neighbor."

When the cubs complained to Papa about Miz McGrizz's attic, it turned out that he was even more enthusiastic about the idea than Mama was. "Cubs, I'm proud of you! I think it's grand of you to volunteer to help poor old Miz McGrizz clean her attic."

"But, Papa, we didn't exactly volunteer," said Brother in a small voice.

"Nevertheless," said Papa, "it's a wonderful thing you're doing. I think you may find it interesting. You never know what you might find in an old lady's attic."

"Careful now," said Miz McGrizz. "These steps are rather rickety."

It was Saturday morning and the cubs were following her up to the attic. When they reached the top of the steps, Brother and Sister just stared for a moment.

"Well, here we are," said Miz McGrizz. They were indeed. A strange feeling came over the cubs as they looked at the piles of old things. It was as if they had walked into the middle of her whole life. There was a dressmaker's dummy with half a dress pinned to it. There were old magazines. There was an amazing ship in a bottle.

"Wow!" said Brother. "It has all the rigging!"

"That was my late husband's hobby," explained Miz McGrizz.

"What's this?" asked Sister.

"A radio, of course!" Miz McGrizz said.

"A radio?" said Sister. "It looks like a little cathedral!"

"Do you think it still plays?" asked Brother.

"Let's plug it in and find out," said Miz McGrizz.

Brother plugged it in and turned it on. Music came pouring out of the strange old radio. Rock music! As the cubs stood listening to rock music coming out of a radio that looked like a cathedral, they had the funniest feeling about how time works. It went back into the past and forward into the future—but now it was the present and they had work to do! Papa was right. Miz McGrizz's attic *was* kind of interesting.

Miz McGrizz organized
two really big boxes. One was
marked THROWAWAYS and one
was marked KEEPERS.

"You know," said Brother,
"we're going to have to have a
system if we're ever going to
get this job done."

Miz McGrizz agreed.

Here's what they did. They sat Miz McGrizz in a comfy old chair and brought things for her to decide about. Then she looked at each thing and said "keep it" or "chuck it." But as the morning went on, the cubs began to worry. It seemed to Brother and Sister that she was chucking some pretty interesting things. They were beginning to get an idea.

It was just before lunch when the cubs found some *really* interesting things. "What's this, Miz McGrizz?" asked Sister. "It looks like a really old Bearbie doll—a really, *really* old Bearbie doll."

"That's what it is," she said. "It's the original Bearbie I had when I was a cub."

Then Brother found something in a box of old papers. It was a baseball card. "I can hardly believe my eyes," he said. "This *looks* like the Babe Bruin rookie card!"

"That's probably what it is," said Miz McGrizz. "My late husband was a big Babe Bruin fan."

After lunch in the attic, the cubs told her their idea.

"There's a lot of great stuff in here!" said Brother. "You shouldn't throw it away!"

"But what should I do with it?" she asked.

"Have a garage sale!" said Sister.

"Goodness," said old Miz McGrizz. "I don't know about that. I don't have a garage."

"You have a yard, don't you?" said Brother. "You can have a yard sale!"

And that's what happened. Mama and Papa pitched in and helped. The very next Saturday, Miz McGrizz had one of the most successful yard sales ever held in the neighborhood. Miz McGrizz appreciated the cubs' help very much and wanted to pay them something. But Mama still wouldn't hear of it. She did allow them to accept gifts, however.

Miz McGrizz gave Sister the original Bearbie doll that she had when she was a cub, and she gave Brother the Babe Bruin rookie card!

"Wow!" said Sister.

"Double wow!" said Brother.